Ears and the Secret Song

For Ellie and Lewis

Laid in the earth like grain that sleeps unseen:
Love is come again,
Like wheat that springeth green.

Easter Carol – The Oxford Book of Carols

Text © 1989 Donut Books
Illustrations © 1989 William Geldart

First published 1989 in the U.K. by Hodder and Stoughton

This edition published 1995 by
Wm. B. Eerdmans Publishing Co.
255 Jefferson Ave. S.E., Grand Rapids, Michigan 49503
All rights reserved

Printed in Belgium by Proost International Book Production

00 99 98 97 96 95   7 6 5 4 3 2 1

ISBN 0-8028-5110-X

EARS *and the* SECRET SONG

Meryl Doney

Illustrated by **William Geldart**

WILLIAM B. EERDMANS PUBLISHING COMPANY
GRAND RAPIDS, MICHIGAN

The very first time Ears the harvest mouse
opened her eyes, she saw the wheat.
Great, green ears, waving across the blue
sky in the bright sun.

Of course, she didn't know it was wheat.
She didn't know anything at all.

Ears scrambled out of the wriggling ball
of fur which was her brothers and sisters.
She poked her nose out of the round nest
and gazed at the bright-as-new colours.
The world looked a very beautiful place.

It didn't take long for the baby mice to grow strong. Their fur grew thick and their tails long. Soon they were bounding around the nest and running up wheat stalks as if they were ladders!

'Look at me,' squeaked Ears'
brother, running up the tallest
wheat stalk. Suddenly it bent in
the middle and he swung down
to the ground, shouting
'Wheeeeee', at the top of his
voice.

'Let's have a go!' shouted
Ears.

She clambered up the stalk
and went wheeeeee . . . BOMP,
right into a clump of thistles!

The spring days sped by as the mice played follow-my-leader amongst the wheat and hide-and-seek along the furrows. They even played 'dare' – running out onto the short grass where they knew there were dangers.

When it was Ears' turn to dare, she dashed out onto the grassy bank.

The next moment everything went dark.

'Where am I?' squealed Ears. 'Where is everyone?'
Far above her, she could see a small circle of light. She scrambled towards it.

'There you are!' came six mice voices, as her head popped out into the sunlight again. 'Were you hiding?'
'No,' said Ears. 'I fell in a hole!'

Most of all, the mice liked being with Mother. She showed them where to find juicy green shoots to nibble. They had lessons in pouncing on beetles and once they had a feast of birds' eggs.

Mother taught them the ways of the other animals, large and small; how to read the sky for signs of rain and how to gather seeds to store for winter.

And she taught them the secret song,
passed from mouse to mouse, for as long
as could be remembered:

I am small and brown, in the earth I lie;
I spring tall and golden, waving at the sky.

   'What does it mean?' whispered the
mice.
   'Live long and you will know,' said
Mother with a smile.

Summer came and the green wheat turned gold in the sun. The mice ran and jumped in the tall stalks, eating their fill of the plump grains and squeaking at the tops of their voices.

One morning Ears woke early. She felt strange. A little shiver ran along her back. She listened hard.

A new sound was mixed with the lark's morning song. A whining, beating sound, like many birds' wings.

All the mice heard it. They began running nervously along the wheat stalks, the way they did when a storm was coming.

Suddenly, the noise grew to a roar. A terrible monster reared up from the wheat, smashing down everything in its path, and chewing it up. The mice were terrified. They clung to the swaying wheat stalks, unable to move.

At the last moment, Ears gave a mighty leap and ran for her life.

Ears stopped, panting, at the top of a bank. Below her the whole world lay broken and ruined by the monster. The golden wheat was gone.

Thick black smoke was curling upwards from the field. The sun grew orange in the sky and suddenly, flickering along the furrows came that oldest enemy of all living creatures — fire.

Ears sat watching its red tongues licking along the furrows until finally, tired and miserable, she fell asleep.

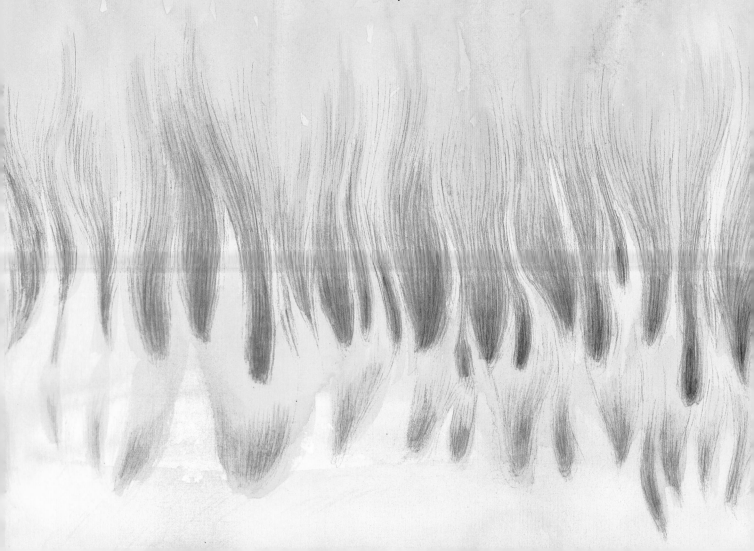

When she woke, it was grey morning. The grass was wet with dew and the air nipped cold. Below her the field lay blackened and bare. Along the brown earth she could see the scattered grains of golden wheat.

Into her mind came the words of the secret song: *'I am small and brown, in the earth I lie . . .'* It reminded her of her mother. Ears began to cry.

As the cool yellow sun came up, Ears
remembered her mother's instructions
about preparing a nest and collecting
food for the winter. She found an empty
rabbit hole and peeped in. It looked
safe and dry, so she set to work to
make a cosy nest.

For the rest of the day she was busy
gathering nuts and seeds to store away.

That night she ate as much as she possibly could, curled up into a ball and fell asleep.

Several times during the long winter Ears dreamed she was
running and jumping amongst the golden wheat. But when she
woke and looked about her, the world was cold and grey. There
were no signs of the wheat grains on the earth.

'Was it all a dream?' she wondered.

Then, one morning, Ears woke with a start. She had been dreaming about the terrible fire, but there was no fire. Instead the sun was streaming into the burrow, warming her and bringing with it the faintest smell of flowers.

Ears scrambled out of her nest and looked over the field. As far as she could see, in every direction, new green shoots were pushing up through the bare earth.

Ears' heart skipped a beat.

'It's come back,' she cried. 'The wheat has come back.'

The words of the secret song jumped into her mind:

I am small and brown, in the earth I lie;
I spring tall and golden, waving at the sky.

'It's about the wheat,' gasped Ears, understanding at last. 'It didn't die. It's going to be golden again!'

Day by day the sun's heat grew stronger and the wheat grew taller. One by one the mice crept out of their winter hiding places. They remembered when they were baby mice. Once again they ran and jumped and played games.

When the sun overhead seemed so large that it would burn her up, Ears began to build a cool nest among the wheat stalks.

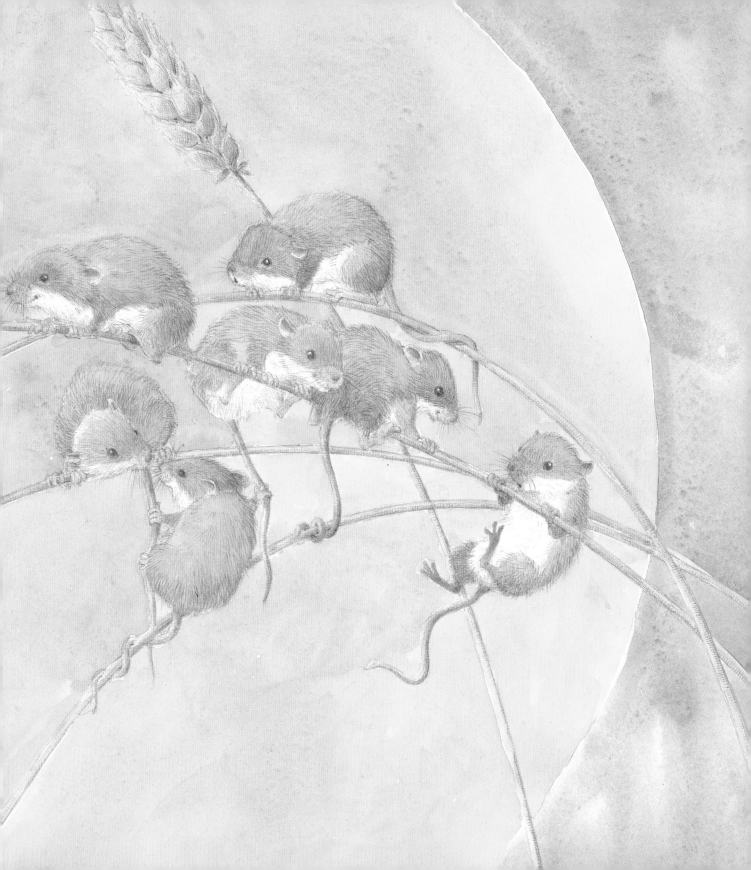

On the very day she finished building, her babies were born. Now there were baby mice to run and jump around her. Ears watched them happily. Together they would explore the world. She would teach them everything she knew.

And she would make sure they knew the secret song, passed from mouse to mouse for as long as could be remembered.

I am small and brown, in the earth I lie;
I spring tall and golden, waving at the sky.

'When they ask me what it means,' thought Ears, looking at the golden wheat and smiling to herself, 'I'll say, "Live long and you will know!"'